HELPING YOUR BRAND-NEW READER

Here's how to make first-time reading easy and fun:

▶ Read the introduction at the beginning of the book aloud. Look through the pictures together so that your child can see what happens in the story before reading the words.

▶ Read the first page to your child, placing your finger under each word.

▶ Let your child touch the words and read the rest of the story. Give him or her time to figure out each new word.

▶ If your child gets stuck on a word, you might say, *"Try something. Look at the picture. What would make sense?"*

▶ If your child is still stuck, supply the right word. This will allow him or her to continue to read and enjoy the story. You might say, *"Could this word be 'ball'?"*

▶ Always praise your child. Praise what he or she reads correctly, and praise good tries too.

▶ Give your child lots of chances to read the story again and again. The more your child reads, the more confident he or she will become.

▶ Have fun!

Copyright © 2000 by Kathy Caple

All rights reserved.

First edition 2000

Library of Congress Cataloging-in-Publication Data
is available.

Library of Congress Catalog Card Number: 00-030403

ISBN 0-7636-1146-8

2 4 6 8 10 9 7 5 3 1

Printed in Hong Kong

This book was typeset in Letraset Arta.
The illustrations were done in watercolor and pen.

Candlewick Press
2067 Massachusetts Avenue
Cambridge, Massachusetts 02140

WELL DONE, WORM!

CANDLEWICK PRESS
CAMBRIDGE, MASSACHUSETTS

WRITTEN AND ILLUSTRATED BY Kathy Caple

Contents

Drip Drip Drip   1

Worm Is Stuck   11

Worm Smells   21

Worm Paints   31

DRIP DRIP DRIP

1

Introduction

This story is called *Drip Drip Drip*.
It's about how the rain drips and drips,
and Worm gets more and more buckets
until there are no more drips. Guess what
Worm will do with all the water.

Drip.

Worm gets a bucket.

Drip drip drip.

6

Worm gets more buckets.

Drip drip drip drip drip.

7

8

Worm gets more and more buckets.

"No more drips!" says Worm.

"Water for sale!" says Worm.

WORM IS STUCK

11

Introduction

This story is called *Worm Is Stuck.*
It's about all the shapes Worm turns
himself into, and what happens when
he ties himself in a knot.

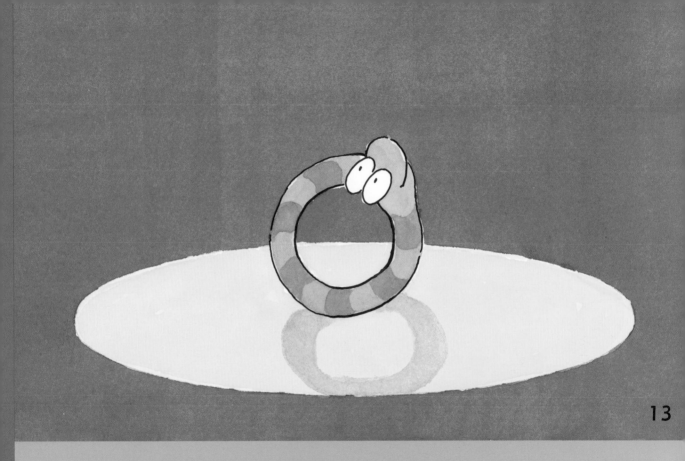

Worm is a circle.

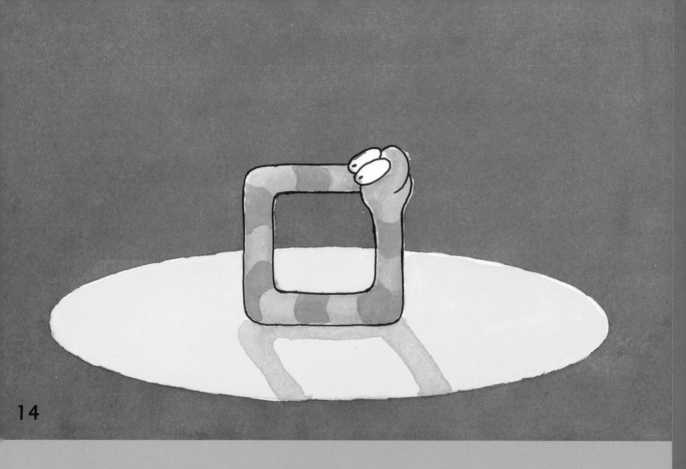

Worm is a square.

Worm is a triangle.

Worm is a zigzag.

Worm is a figure eight.

18

Worm is a bow.

Worm is a knot.

Worm is stuck.

WORM SMELLS

Introduction

This story is called *Worm Smells.*
It's about all the things that Worm sees
and smells on his walk. Some things smell
nice, but one thing smells bad!

Worm sees a flower.

sniff

"Smells nice," says Worm.

Worm sees a pine cone.

sniff

"Smells nice," says Worm.

Worm sees a strawberry.

sniff

"Smells nice," says Worm.

Worm sees a skunk.

"Smells bad!" says Worm.

WORM PAINTS

Introduction

This story is called *Worm Paints.*
It's about how Worm paints pictures that
Rat and Turtle and Frog don't like. Then
Worm paints a picture they all love.

Worm paints a picture.

"I don't like it," says Rat.

Worm paints a picture.

"I don't like it," says Turtle.

Worm paints a picture.

"I don't like it," says Frog.

Worm paints a picture.

"We love it!" they all say.